Boots for Toots

written and illustrated by

Miriam Macdonald

Ready to Read

Learning Media
Wellington

These boots are too big.

These boots are too small.

These boots are too long.

These boots are too tall.

These boots are too wide.

These boots are too tight.

These boots are just right.